LORD
IN
THE
CONCORDE

Cormac G. McDermott, BA, MEconSc.

Order this book online at www.trafford.com
or email orders@trafford.com

Most Trafford titles are also available at major online book retailers.

Print information available on the last page.

ISBN: 978-1-4907-9943-8 (sc)
ISBN: 978-1-4907-9944-5 (e)

Trafford rev. 01/22/2020

www.trafford.com
North America & international
toll-free: 1 888 232 4444 (USA & Canada)
fax: 812 355 4082

CONTENTS

CHAPTER 1

THE CRAIC IN THE CONC

SCENE FROM THE CONCORDE LOUNGE & BAR IN EDENMORE, RAHENY ON THE NORTH SIDE OF DUBLIN – SEVERAL MEN ASSOCIATED WITH ST. MALACHY'S ASSOCIATION FOOTBALL CLUB HAVE ARRANGED TO MEET UP FOR A FEW PINTS DURING JANUARY, 2016. CORMAC IS THE FIRST IN THE PUB AND IS WAITING FOR HIS PALS TO ARRIVE. A COUPLE OF THEM WALK IN.

CORMAC: 'Alright, fellas'.

HOBBSER: 'Howayeh, Cormac'.

THEY SHAKE HANDS.

JOE: 'Alright, mate. What are you having, Hobbser?'

HOBBSER: 'Gerruz a cider, please'.

JOE: 'Cormac, are you alright for a gargle?'

CORMAC: 'I'm grand for the moment, thanks'.

JOE GOES UP TO THE BAR.

HOBBSER: 'Are you off the drink?'

CORMAC: 'I'm just having a few blackcurrants. Going to try
and take it easy for a few weeks. I drank a lot during
December because of my birthday and Christmas.
Watching my funds too'.

HOBBSER: 'Fair play to yeh'.

JOE COMES BACK FROM THE BAR WITH THE DRINKS.
HOBBSER IS LOOKING AT HIS MOBILE PHONE.

CORMAC: 'How's your new job going, Joe?'

JOE: 'Ah, it's grand. I'm not in 'til ten in the morning.
Normally I start at seven. Half nine for the rest of
the week. Put on a later shift'.

CORMAC: 'What time will you finish at?'

JOE: 'Seven'.

CORMAC: 'What exactly is it you do?'

JOE: 'I'm working on a machine that cuts cables and stuff.
You know the big massive ones used in construction
and that?'

CORMAC: 'Oh, right. You've done a few different jobs over the
last while now, haven't you?'

JOE: 'I have'.

CORMAC: 'Fair play to you. You obviously just want to work'.

JOE: 'Ah, yeah'.

CORMAC: 'Hey, Hobbser. You wouldn't mind looking up the latest scores from the Dutch league for me, would you?'

HOBBSER: 'Have you something next door?'

CORMAC: 'Yeah, did a five euro accumulator?'

HOBBSER: 'Who are you looking for?'

CORMAC: 'How are Feyenoord getting on?'

HOBBSER: 'They won two nil'.

CORMAC: 'Ah, great'.

JOE: 'How many more results are you waiting to come up?'

CORMAC: 'Another eight'.

HOBBSER: 'Jayziz. How much will that be worth to you?'

CORMAC: 'Ah, just eighty eight euro'.

JOE: 'On a nine game accumulator?'

HOBBSER: 'You must have gone with all the favourites?'

CORMAC: 'Yeah, short odds on most of them'.

THE FIRST GAME OF THE AFTERNOON STARTS. AN INCIDENT OCCURS.

HOBBSER: 'That looked like a penalty to me'.

CORMAC: 'It did to me too. Hold on and we'll see the replays'.

JOE: 'No, I think the 'keeper made contact with the ball'.

HOBBSER: 'He got the man if you ask me'.

CORMAC: 'I agree. You're the one wearing the glasses, mate'!

JOE: 'You need a pair'!

CORMAC: 'Why don't you grow them?'!

THEY ALL LAUGH.

WELSHER WALKS IN.

WELSHER: 'Are you on the dry there, Cormac?'

CORMAC: 'Yeah, taking it handy for the moment, pal. Hey, Hobbser. How are Ajax doing?'

HOBBSER: 'They won three one'.

A WHILE LATER. THE FIRST GAME HAS FINISHED. A NUMBER MORE FRIENDS HAVE ARRIVED AND THE PUB IS FAIRLY PACKED.

GERRY: 'I hope the Liverpool fans don't light any flares if they score today'.

CORMAC: 'Yeah, they've done it a few times at Old Trafford over the last couple of seasons, haven't they?'

WELSHER: 'I saw less 'flares' back in the Seventies'!

THEY ALL CHUCKLE.

HOBBSER: 'Sorry, Cormac, but I've gone against yiz today'.

CORMAC: 'What do you mean?'

HOBBSER: 'Did draw at half time, United to win'.

JOE: 'What price did you get on that?'

HOBBSER: '7/2. I hope it's a draw anyway'.

GERRY: 'It would benefit Spurs'.

HOBBSER: 'That's right'!

WELSHER: 'Here comes Truckee. I thought he was barred out of here?'

GERRY: 'I think he's on his final warning'.

JOE: 'I reckon it's a three-strikes-and-you're-out thing'.

HOBBSER: 'Should be saying that to the Luas drivers in the run-up to the centenary of the Easter Rising'!

CORMAC: 'He does get troublesome with a few gargles on him'.

GERRY: 'He's an alcoholic'.

CORMAC: 'You'd feel a bit sorry for him so'.

JOE: 'The dipso has picked up more 'pints' since August than what Man Utd have done in the whole of the Premier League era'!

HOBBSER: 'The Turkish bloke yiz got in the transfer window this month could make his debut today, Joe'.

GERRY: 'Oh, Mustafa Babacan'.

CORMAC: 'Sounds like what blokes back in the Eighties would have said if they wanted to drink and drive'!

JOE: 'It's what Truckee should be thinking to himself'!

HOBBSER: 'Jayziz, the Eighties. Remember all those pirate radio stations back then. The music was great though'.

GERRY: 'It's regarded as the greatest ever era in music'.

CORMAC: 'What about all the political incorrectness'!

JOE: 'Yeah, you'd never get away with it today'.

HOBBSER: 'I was tuning in one time when I was about sixteen and a deejay was getting well p*ssed off'.

CORMAC: 'What do you mean?'

HOBBSER: 'He was about to finish his show, but the bloke that was supposed to be on after him hadn't yet shown up'.

JOE: 'H'har har. What did he say?'!

HOBBSER: 'Flakey Scalp is on after nine to take yiz into the small hours. Datz if eeh boddaws tih tuhrn up (That's if he bothers to turn up)'!

CORMAC: 'So professional! Diss iz yaw trebbill teeh aw (This your TTTR)'!

THEY ALL CRACK UP.

WELSHER: 'What are those small boats in the ad called again?'

GERRY: 'Sampans'.

WELSHER: 'Is that, that Pistol Pete fella?'!

CORMAC: 'Ah, Welsher. Will ya stop'!

JOE: 'Funny the Far East should come up. Was walking down the Tonlegee Road the other day and saw a make of car called a Suzuki Jimny. Never saw one of those before'.

HOBBSER: 'Jimny? Is that what Japanese kids with hare lips think Santa Claus comes down when delivering the Xmas presents?'!

ED COMES IN AND SITS NEXT TO CORMAC.

ED: 'Howayeh, pal. Did a super yankee earlier. One of me horses is running in the next race'.

CORMAC: 'What's it called?'

ED: 'Raifteiri. Think it's something to do with that Italian bloke who's leading Leicester to the Premier League this season'!

CORMAC: 'H'har har! Some horses have interesting names, ey? Saw one the other day. Zebedaios he was called. What you'd get if you crossed The Magic Roundabout and a Greek island, right?'!

ED: 'Very good'!

CORMAC: 'Know next to nothing about horse racing. What I've spotted is that in a race meeting with seven on the card, about two favourites win. You're better off not betting on the favourite'!

ED CHUCKLES.

CORMAC: 'I was watching a race one time and in my head picked out a horse called Wagon Eva and it won. If I was bitter, I'd believe God was being cruel, but if I am committed to forgiving, I can look upon it as a blessing and He's was just trying to heal a wound as we all have to accept he is always in control and we should bet with our heart if we do so'!

ED LOOKS A BIT CONFUSED.

ED: 'If that's the way you see things, mate. I go with the trainers and jockeys'.

CORMAC: 'That's why you win a lot I suppose'.

ED: 'Got three grand on a super yankee one December. Had a great Christmas out of that I tell yeh. I'd like to think I know the form dih yeh know worroy meein (do you know what I mean)?'

CORMAC: 'I love the creatures and am intrigued by the names their owners give to them. Saw one last Summer that won the Epsom derby called Harzand. Must be 'lord of the jungle' aswell or something'!

ED: 'Jayziz. H'har har'!

CORMAC: 'Around the same time I saw another one called Hubertas. What you'd get if you crossed Opportunity Knocks and an Eighties Fiat car, ey?!

ED: 'You're on 'form' today dih yeh know worroy meein?'

CORMAC: 'Talking about cars, saw a Volkswagen Tigaun the other day. What you'd get if you crossed an Indian leaf picker and an Argentinian footballer'!

ED: 'Any mohwhawh (Any more)?'

CORMAC: 'Yeah, talking about Indians and horses, saw a nag by the name of Birikyno one time. Cross between and meal from the sub-continent and an ex-Man U captain from Cork, right?'!

ED SMILES.

CORMAC: 'And talking about horses and Argentinians, there was another nag by the name of Bin Battuta. That one's a cross between a Muslim refuse collector and an ex-Argentinian striker! Dih yeh know worroy meein?'!

ED: 'Keep gohwhin'.

CORMAC: 'Let me see. Orcia was a horse I saw last Summer aswell. That's that killer whale that got revenge on Richard Harris in a flick a few decades back'!

ED: 'Yiv lost me dayaw (You've lost me there)'.

CORMAC: 'Spotted one, one time named McKinley. Apparently it's some 'mount' according to Coors Light drinkers'!

ED: 'Is there any end to this?'!

CORMAC: 'Mandatario. Sounds like a strict stipulation in a Canadian state, ey?! Chipciu, like getting the DART to a casino after eating a large single'!

ED GIGGLES:

CORMAC: 'Or what about Janchies? That sounds like a baseball team from New York or maybe the Dutch bloke who invented edam'! And Durica. What the bloke who invented the battery said'!

ED: 'Do you think up any jokes about the football?'

CORMAC: 'Sometimes. Once heard a pundit say 'quelle gashi'. It's French for 'what a mess'. So I thought to myself does that mean 'quelle messi' means 'what a gash' if the little b*llix was to continue running rings around your defence and what injury he should pick up on his ankle by your ruthless left-full'!

ED: 'Any what about his team-mates?'

CORMAC: 'Rakatic makes me think of the Spanish Inquisition'!

ED: 'Oi'm confeeooizzed (I'm confused)'.

CORMAC: 'Yeah, 'rack a titch', but leave the six footers alone as they are already tall enough was their attitude by all accounts'!

ED SMILES.

CORMAC: 'And some other bloke. Arda. Called after a chalice. Can't imagine he has a colleague called Derrynaflan though'!

ED: 'Jayziz'.

CORMAC: 'Saw something else by the name Roksanda. That's the drink you get when you mix orange and lemon'!

ED: 'You're gas! Alright, oi'm gowin ohvawh tih tawlk tih Jer forrah biht (Alright, I'm going over here to talk to Jer for a bit)'.

CORMAC: 'Okay, no probs'.

CORMAC TURNS BACK TO THE GROUP.

JOE: 'A lot of those Liverpool and United fans just abuse each other. Was at a game between them one time and was in the away end near where they're segregated. There was a few who spent the whole match just shouting abuse at each other. They weren't even watching the game'.

HOBBSER: 'There's good and bad on both sides'.

CORMAC: 'Of course there is, but people are responsible for their own actions. However, if you are not fundamentally-inclined, then you must respect that there can be aspects of your behaviour that can bring out things in others that they may not want to come out with out of their own volition'!

JOE: 'Ah, would ya ever stop talking deep sh*te, Cormac'!

CORMAC CHUCKLES.

GERRY: 'You and Ed where talking for a while. He was laughing. Go on, tell us the joke'.

CORMAC: 'Ah, I was just cracking stuff about the names of horses and things'.

JOHN: 'Give us an example. It might ease the tension before the big game kicks off'.

CORMAC: 'I was watching At The Races one day and spotted a nag called Morzine. Is that, that stuff they give people who are under the care of a palliative team?'!

SOME OF THEM LAUGH BUT IT TAKES A BIT LONGER TO REGISTER WITH OTHERS.

HOBBSER: 'You're great craic and you're not even drinking'.

CORMAC: 'Thanks, mate'.

JOE: 'You were a beer monster back in your twenties I was told'!

CORMAC: 'When I was a student on working holidays in the States, I reckon I did more 'bongs' than the history of the Angelus alright'!

CORMAC GETS UP AND GOES TO THE TOILET.

GERRY: 'I'm telling yiz lads, we could be seriously affected by this whole Brexit thing that's happening in the U.K.'.

JOE: 'Ah, Brexit me arse. If Brexit was to exit, then the stay campaign could have been called Bray'!

HOBBSER: 'What will it be called if they want to get back in? Bre-entrance'!

THE CONVERSATIONS CONTINUE AS THE ACTION IN THE GAME PLAYS OUT.

ANOTHER SCENE FROM THE CONCORDE LOUNGE IN EDENMORE, RAHENY ON THE NORTH SIDE OF DUBLIN. UNUSUALLY ENOUGH, THE LADS HAVE CONGREGATED TO HAVE A FEW DRINKS WHILE A GAME OF FOOTBALL IS BEING SHOWN LIVE ON TELEVISION!

JER: 'Don't recognise yaw man der. Who's he?'

DEVO: 'Massaro'.

JER: 'Where did dey gerrim from?'

HAGGIS: 'Maybe somewhere in India coz he sounds like he's named after that chicken tikka dish'!

THE GROUP LAUGH.

CORMAC: 'Hey, Haggis. See dat Srna fella?'

HAGGIS: 'Yeah'.

CORMAC: 'Starship, Phil Lynott and Fleetwood Mac sang about dat girl, didn't dey?'!

HAGGIS: 'I actually thought it's what Scousers call a sandwich'!

JER: 'A sarnie you mean, Haggis'.

HOBBSER: 'Is he a fab sarnie, Jer?'!

CORMAC: 'Fab sarnie? That was a comedy show all about World War II on the BBC about forty years ago, right?'!

THERE'S A COLLECTIVE 'JAYZIZ' FROM THE MEN.

JER: 'Don't be takin' the Lord's name in vain lads'.

CORMAC: 'I think your man Brosnovic is that bloke from Meath who played 007 a few years back'!

HAGGIS: 'Put that next in your next book, Cormac'.

CORMAC: 'Maybe I will, Haggis'.

HAGGIS: 'Don't put me in it. Just give us a copy as they come in handy for balancing the coffee table'!

CORMAC: 'How many times have I got to tell ya, I get good professional reviews for my work?'

HAGGIS: 'Professional what? Watch makers! None of my gags better be in there, I'll be looking for royalties off yeh'.

CORMAC: 'I've told you before I write all my own work. Your jokes are not good enough anyway'.

HAGGIS: 'Now, now, The Author'!

HOBBSER: 'Tried cous cous on a salad for the first time earlier. Nice, but a bit dry'.

HAGGIS: 'He's that Hungarian legend who scored all those goals for Real Madrid in the Sixties. Put that in yaw book, Cormac'!

CORMAC (Laughing): 'Yeah, maybe I will, mate'! Rosiscky, the number ten in white. Sounds like a word used to describe gambling on volatile stock markets in the Czech Republic!

DEVO: 'Datz brutal. You needn't try and sell me a copy either, Cormac'!

CORMAC: 'Modric? Two words you could use to describe Paul Weller, particularly after all the royalties from 'A Town Called Malice'!

CHARLIE: 'Ah, will ya shurrup owadah'!

CORMAC: 'No, I won't, Charlie! As for Hutnik, 'Something's Got Me Started', dat's dat rocket the Soviet Union sent into space back in the late Sixties, isnt it?'!

HAGGIS
(Talking to
one of the
barmen):
'Mooch, don't serve him any mohwhawh! Anyway, daw couldn't be more 'itches' if daw wives said 'I want to have yaw scabies"!

EDDIE WALKS IN.

ED
(Talking to
Cormac):
'H'hey, The Mac is back'!

CORMAC: 'Hey, Ed. Yaw man Erkin der had dat big green building in The City in London named after him, didn't he?!

ED: 'Yiv lost me, Cormac. Heeaw, Ciara, stick us on a pint will yeh?'

CORMAC: See dah fella, Priskian, lads. Datz what you'd call a Hungarian person who believes in Jesus'!

JER: 'Datz not funny, Cormac'.

BERNIE: 'Will yiz leave him alone'.

GERRY: 'Plenty of room down der, Cormac'!

CORMAC: 'I'm well used to yeh saying that by now'!

GERRY LAUGHS.

CORMAC: 'As for yaw man, Dzsudzsaks, is dat what you'd describe people from Dublin who celebrate the Sabbath of a Saturday?!

JER: 'Datz not funny making fun of religion, Cormac. I'm surprised at you'.

WILLIE: 'Don't be casting dispersions'!

BERNIE: 'Don't mind dim, Cormac'.

LOUISE: 'Der all ferals'!

CORMAC: 'Give over eating the statues, Jer'!

JER: 'I'm not. You eat dim too'.

CORMAC
(Sarcastically):   'I do alright'.

HAGGIS: 'Yih wouldn't want to be losing yaw saltiness quicker dan boiled ham either, would yeh doh?'!

THEY ALL LAUGH...INCLUDING CORMAC.

CORMAC: 'Ilsanker, in blue. Ders a kebab shop on Dame Street by dat name owned by snooker players with sclerosis of the liver'!

JER: 'No more gags, Cormac. Whawh rawll watching de game (We're all watching the game)'.

WELSHER: 'Don't mind dim, Cormac. I'm getting a laugh owrovyeh (out of you). Heeaw, Mooch, throw us on an auld Jayziz pint eh Guinness owadah, will yeh?'.

THE ULLA: 'Ah, will yiz kah mahn (Ah, will you come on)'!

THINGS SETTLE DOWN AND THEY CONCENTRATE ON THE ACTION WITH THE ODD COMMENT ABOUT IT HERE AND THERE UNTIL HALF-TIME ARRIVES.

WELSHER: 'Yaw obviously still going for yaw walks, Cormac. Saw yeh on the Tonlegee dee uddaw day'.

CORMAC: 'Ah, I must average sixty kilometers a week. Spotted a car in Cameron Estate with IFSDC.com on one of the windows. Wonder what darriz'.

HAGGIS: 'It's probably the financial services centre in Washington'!

THEY CHUCKLE AND CONTINUE TO CHAT UNTIL THE GAME RE-STARTS.

CORMAC: 'Shaqiri? Is he anything to dat girl who sang 'Hips Don't Lie?'

HAGGIS (Throwing his eyes up): 'Aw, good night'.

HOBBSER: 'Yer man Salvado could be dat bloke who couldn't score for Super Spurs a few years back'!

THEY ALL GIGGLE...INCLUDING CORMAC.

WELSHER: 'Lagerback? Does he have an alcoholic brother called 'Knocking The' who's a right p*sshead altogether'!

CORMAC: 'As for Cahill, datz dat island just off our west coast dat dyslexics can't pronounce properly, right?'!

WELSHER (Imitating Cormac): 'Yeah, yeah, yeah'!

CORMAC: 'They can't pronounce it properly alright, teamy'!

HOBBSER: 'Kane has had a very disappointing tournament'!

HAGGIS: 'His namesake, Michael, would have done a lot better'!

CORMAC: 'And a lot of people DO know dat'!

THE BANTER CONTINUES AS THEY WATCH THE MATCH.

CHAPTER 2

DEM TWO ARSEH*LES

Paddy and Mick are drinking a few cans in Paddy's gaff. 'Wud jeh moyinnd tuhrnin awn de futbawll, Paddee (Would you mind turning on the football, Paddy)?', says Mick. 'Yeah, no probs', replies Paddy. 'Who's playing?, he continues. 'Bahzill argh hohstin Krisstill Palliss in eh Yuhrohpeh Leeigg match (Basel are hosting Crystal Palace in a Europa League match)', Mick answers. Paddy asks 'Whawh skawrzz eht (What score is it)?'. 'Itz wawhn-awll aht deh mohminnt. Kahn yeh nawht seedeh kaptchin in deh tawp left ov deh screeinn (It's one-all @ the moment. Can you not see the caption in the top left of the screen)?', Mick inquires. 'Oh, roight (Oh, right)', says he. 'Jayziz, oi tawht daht wazz inn ahdd fawh Skoy Spawrtz Tawmmee Hillfiggawh (Jayziz, I thought that was an ad for Sky Sports Tommy Hilfiger)'!

Paddy and Mick were watching the international football during the Summer of 2019. Says Paddy 'See dah roight full faw Pawrtjewgill (See that right full for Portugal)?'. 'Yeah', replies Mick. 'Oi tink he had a sandwich named aftawh rim'. (I think he had a sandwich named after him).'Whawh jeh meein (What do you mean)?', asks Mick. 'A baykinn, lerrisse and SEMEDO wawhn' (A bacon, lettuce and tomato one), quips Paddy. 'Whawh rabbowht diss felleh cummin' awn faw Oirelint (What about this fella coming on for Ireland)?', asks Mick. 'Hooh, Joxer Manley (Who, Joxer Manley)?', enquires Paddy. 'Yeah' and he continues 'Hooizz heeh wiht (Who's he with)?'.

'Oi dowhinn knowh, burr eez so owilld oi rekkin eez wiht dee AA faw dee inseeoordince awn eez zimmaw frayimm (I don't know, but he's so old I reckon he's with the AA for the insurance on his zimmer frame)', cracks Paddy!

Paddy and Mick are drinking a few cans together. 'Whawh dih yeh mayke ih diss Brexit sho*te (What do you make of this Brexit sh*te)?', says Paddy. 'Datz de furhst meal ih didday, izzin eht (That's the first meal of the day, isn't it)?', replies Mick. Says Paddy 'Well, we do have Brunch oi suppohwhizz. Whawh wud jeh tink eh Brinner den (Well, we do have Brunch I suppose. What do you think of Brinner then?)'. 'He woz in 'De King Ann Oi', wazzin eeh (He was in 'The King And I', wasn't he)?', answers Mick. He continues, 'How do yeh feeill bowht Brea ye tick (How do you feel about Brea ye thick)?'. 'Eevin cheeseeawh dan de French 'Pixie & Dixie'' (Even cheesier than the French 'Pixie & Dixie'), Paddy jokes. Asks Mick, 'Woi dohwhin yeh just mooiv awhn teh Brupper den (Why don't you just move on to Brupper then)?'. 'Datz daht prohgramme awhn Channill 4 all bowht eh 'Big' wawhn whehr young peepill live in eh howhiss tigeddawh ann gerrup tih awhll sawhrts, roight (That's that programme on Channel 4 all about a 'Big' one where young people live in a house together and get up to all sorts right)?', he retorts. 'Well, yid wawhnt teh gerrah 'Big Brupper' inteh yeh awllroight coz de next day yih cud be f*cked as oi've been heerdin tings bowht eh no-meal Brexit inn awll daht' (Well, you'd want to get a 'Big Brupper' into you alright because the next day you could be f*cked as I've been hearing things about a no-meal Brexit and all that), quips Mick. Both men laugh!

Mick and Paddy are watching television during mid-July. 'Wotz diss?', asks Paddy. 'Itz ahn Ardinge perayidd (It's an Orange parade)', replies Mick. 'Tiddayh izz De Twelft (Today is The Twelfth)', he continues. Voice from the television: 'Nobody should be offended by this parade, we are just celebrating our Protestant culture. These marches should be viewed as pageants'. 'Padjintzz (Pageants)?', says Paddy. 'Are dey dohwhizz burdz daht floy back tih East Belfast from long disstinsiz ind say 'Coo coo' (Are those birds that fly back to East Belfast from long distances and say 'Coo coo')?', he says wittily!

Dem two arseh*les are out on a walk in a local park. Paddy tells Mick, 'Oi'm just bahck from de sun havvin' been on holiday in Lahnzirrorreeh wiht de missus (I'm just back from the sun having been on holiday in Lanzarote with the missus)'. 'Aw, roight', answers Mick while deep in thought. 'Oi woz in Puerta del Carmen meself wiht de wyiff a feooh yeeaws ago. Whawh pahrt ih dee oylindt wehr yooh awn?' (I was in Puerta del Carmen myself with the wife a few years ago. What part of the island were you on?)'. 'Ozorla', answers Paddy. 'Oi tawht daht was daht blowk hooh playid futbawll faw Ahrsenill a woyill bahck and hazz kinnect chinz tih Krissmiss' (I thought that was that bloke who played football for Arsenal a while back, and has connections to Christmas'), says Mick!

Paddy and Mick are listening to the radio. Paddy comments that he loves the music of Glenn Campbell. Asks Mick, 'Whawht wud be yaw fayvreht sawng ih hizz (What would be you favourite song of his)?'. 'Oi tink irrid havteh be 'Boi De Tyim Oi Geht Tih Feenix' (I think it would have to be 'By The Time I Get To Phoenix')', answers Paddy. He continues 'Dahr Albehkerrkee izz eh funnee sowindin nayim fawreh playss, izzin eht (That Albuquerque is a funny sounding name for a place, isn't it)?'. 'Datz de nayim ovveh sirreeh? Feck me, oi tawht datz whawht yid geht iff yih happind teh scawr eh hohwhill in wawhn awn eh per fyiv (That's the name of a city. Feck me, I thought that's what you'd get if you happened to score a hole in one on a par five)'!

The two men are having a pint in their local. 'Hey, Paddy?', says Mick. 'Yuhr nayim izz veree commin, izzin eht? (Your name is common, isn't it?)', he continues. 'Yeah', he answers. 'Durz eh lorreh Paddy Kelly's owht dayaw awlroyht. Worr ebowht yooh? Durz eh gud feeooh Mick Murphy's tooh, izzin daw? (There's a lot of Paddy Kelly's out there alright. What about you? There's a good few Mick Murphy's too, isn't there?)', he asks rhetorically. 'Seeuhr izz (Sure is)', Mick acknowledges. 'Jeh noh whawh, durz tree Browinnzz awn de Gahrdinnzz (Do you what, there's three Brown's on the Gardens)', he adds. 'F*ck me, Mick, yid be fawgivvin faw wundordin iff diss izz Dublin awh Cleveland soh, ey (F*ck me, Mick, you'd be forgiven for wondering if this is Dublin or Cleveland so, ey)?'! They bellow!

Paddy and Mick are enjoying a few cans while watching sport in Mick's gaff. 'Jayziz, diss oice hawckee izz eh daynjurriss gayim awltiggedawh (Jayziz, this ice hockey is a dangerous game altogether)', Paddy deduces. 'Irriz', agrees Mick. 'Deev alorreh funnee nayims tooh, mayhte (They've a lot of funny names too, mate)', he adds. 'Wotz daht blowhke in gohwhill cawlld (What's that bloke in goal called)?', Mick enquires. 'Mosley', replies Paddy. 'Oi asskd yeh eez nayim nawht whawht koyinnd eh seeree-ell he had fawh breckfist (I asked you his name not what kind of cereal he has for his breakfast)', quips Mick while chuckling. Paddy retorts, 'Soyidd ih deh mowht w*hnkaw (Side of the mouth w*nker)'!

Yet again, the men meet up. This time they go for a walk towards Dollymount Strand, Bull Island on the north side of Dublin. Paddy notices that there is a wide variety of bird species. 'Yeah, oi noh. Whawhtzz daht whawhn ohvaw dayaw wiht de lawng cuhrvee beek cawlld (Yeah, I know. What's that one over there with the long curvy beek called)?', questions Mick. 'Wheyawh? Aw, yeah. Oi seeh deh whawhn yaw tawlkhin ebbowht. Dahtzz eh cuhrlooh (Where? Aw, yeah. I see the one your talking about. That's a curlew)', he replies. Says Mick humorously, 'Cuhrlooh? Is daht whawht deh law whawhn teh implement fawh dohwhizz littill bahsturdzz hooh cawzz trubill aht noyht (Curlew? Is that what the law want to implement for those little bastards who cause trouble at night)?'! 'Shurrup yooh (Shut up you)', Paddy responds smiling!

The two of them are in a local convenience store at the deli counter one afternoon. 'Worreh dem tings daht look loyhke lirrill peetzehs dayaw, Paddeeh (What are them things that look like little pizzas there, Paddy)?', asks Mick. 'Aw, dohwhizz tings. Dawh cawlld 'jambons', prenowhinnssdd 'kkhahm bowhinzz' (Aw, those things. They are called 'jambons, pronounced 'kham bones')', says Paddy. 'Oi tink itzz deh Spahnisshh fawh hahm (I think it's the Spanish for ham)', he continues. 'Sowhinddzz mawh loyhke eh sexyooilly errowhizzdd jehr eh Chivvawhzz (Sounds more like a sexually aroused jar of Chivers)', Mick wittily blurts! He follows up 'Yooh whawh cawllinn dim jem bawmbs beefowhawh (You were calling them gem bombs before)'! 'Yooh inn yawh f*ckin' jem bawmbs. Ahrr yooh tawhkin' ebbowht yoohzinn explohssivs teh carree owht

26

eh jewillawreeh hoyst nowh ye loonehtick (You and your f*ckin' gem bombs. Are you talking about using explosives to carry out a jewellery heist now you lunatic)?', smarts Paddy!

Paddy and Mick are having a cup of tea and a sandwich in Paddy's kitchen during Summer. Says Paddy, 'Wud jeh moyinnd cuvawrdin up deh rest eh dohwhizz sambohs dayaw, Mick? (Would you mind covering up the rest of those sambos there, Mick?)'. 'Yawr oveeusslee wurreed ebowht deh floyizz gohwhinn errowinnd, mayhte. Daht royht? (You're obviously worried about the flies going around. That right?)', he replies. 'Yeah', says he. 'Deeh yoorinnayht when deeh tayhk awff (They urinate when they take off)'. 'Aw, royht (Aw, right)', says Mick thinking a little deeply. 'Soh when yeh ettahck dim wirreh teeh towhill, deeh p*ss dimselves azz eppoowhizzd teh sh*ttin' dimselves. Veree feckin' cheehkee awv dim awlltiggedawh, ey? (So when you attack them with a tea towel, they p*ss themselves as opposed to sh*ttin' themselves. Very feckin' cheeky of them altogether, ey?)', he funnily concludes!

The two men are going to an international soccer match at the Aviva Stadium on the south side of Dublin one evening. They enter a pub close to the ground and order a couple of pints. 'Hohpp wheeh win diss wawhn tinnoyht, Paddeeh (Hope we win this one tonight, Paddy), says Mick anticipatingly. 'Whawht scawrrh jeh tink iht moyht beeh? (What score do you think it might be?), he continues. 'Oi tink wheel giv dim eh tumpin. Bowht ayht nuhtinn (I think we'll give them a thumping. About eight nothing), answers Paddy. 'Oi tink yuhr loohzzin deh run ih yawself. Ayht nuhtin? (I think you're losing the run of yourself. Eight nothing?), replies he. 'Nawhrr illawll, mayht, oi'm tohtlee cawmpiss menntiss (Not at all, mate, I'm totally compos mentis)', Paddy retorts. 'Ooh, cawmpiss menntiss. Boy deh wheyh, cawmpiss? Dahtzz whawh deh billdinns owht inn U.C.D. ahrr bilt awhn, royht? (Ooh, compos mentis. By the way, compos? That's what the buildings out in U.C.D. are built on, ey?)', laughs Mick. Putting on a D4 accent Paddy reseponds 'Yawh, roysh. Yooh now (Yes, right. You know). The men chuckle, as do some people eavesdropping on their conversation!

Once again, Paddy and Mick meet up for a pint. Says Paddy, 'Dem burdz eh pray can be roight f*ckin' bahsturdz alltiggeddawh (The birds of prey can be right f*ckin' bastards altogether)'. 'Whawh jeh meein? (What do you mean?)', replies Mick. 'Oi hahd sum ih dem beefowawh ind dee whehr grahnnd (I had some of them before and they were grand)', he continues. 'Whawh toypzz? (What types)', inquires Paddy. 'Tooh beegillz (Two beagles)', answers Mick. Being a little curious, Paddy inquires again, 'Did jeh giv dim nayimz? (Did you give them names?)'. 'Yeah', says Mick. 'Wehll, whawh jeh cawll dim den (Well, what did you call them then)?', asks Paddy with great interest. 'Jerrimmee ind Filledelfee-eh (Jeremy and Philadelphia)', quips Mick wittily. Paddy nearly falls off his stool laughing!

CHAPTER 3

JAYZIZ, THAT'S GAS!

Was watching The Bloomberg Channel and their chief Asia analyst said, regarding the stand-off between the U.S. and China, there would be 'Two main take aways' and 'The Chinese would want to come to the table'. Now, may I suggest the U.S. (in order to thaw the ice'berg') bring the required number of Big Mac meals along with them and both parties sort this whole thing out for the benefit of the World economy...and the 'Bloom'ing rest of us too. Honestly!

Saw my cousin's Facebook post about the price of drink in the Temple Bar area of Dublin late 2018. EURO7.90 for a lager. Well, if you think that's bad I read several years back that when a football manager rang another, he was quoted EURO100M for Icardi...just hope in that case (had they bought him) the bottle of cola to come along with him would have at least been on the house!

Puerto Rico played Belize in an international soccer game during November, 2018. Wonder if Gazza's old best mate, Jimmy Five, qualifies to play for the away side because of the ancestral rule?!

Was watching The GOD Channel recently and saw a great preacher and lovely man called Troy Brewer. Just thinking that the European Cup in rugby is sponsored by Heineken afterall and the current holders play at the RDS, the public home of Len's Store who are now four times Champions...but is it by the grace of GOD or because of the braces by BOD...hmmm, roysh!

Watching Man United play Juventus one evening and reckon the scorer of the opening goal (i.e. Dybala) has a brother called Possesso who works as a statistician for Sky Italia and was very happy with his sibling's teams' passing/movement in the first half anyway!

A mate once said that Pele was 'the greatest footballer to have ever have breathed'. I don't know, Paulo Rossi having opened up those two thousand litres of wine he got as a gift after he had scored a hat-trick for Italy during Espana '82 would be right up there with him I reckon!

As I've told you all before, I have prophetic and psychic abilities. One morning, I couldn't for the life of me figure out why The New Avengers was on my mind, but all I will say is that when I walked into The Track, me auldie Charlie 'Purdy' was checking out the prices on the board. This younger fella asked me 'Are you going for the favourite in the next race at Leopardstown? What's it called again?'. 'Absolutely. Flavius', I replied. By this stage, I couldn't decide whether I wanted to get me oats or feed them to the nag, but started humming 'Start the race the Flavius way. The brighter way to start the race. Start the race, get outta Flavius' way. 'Cold Stare' and 'Frosty' are stalling'!

A football legend was quoted as saying something like 'If GOD intended for football not to be played on the ground, He'd have put grass in the air'. Funny that because I heard having got 'Highgarden' to cross the winning post first in the 2:25 at Newmarket one day, the winning jockey was inspired to fly off and take part in a 5-a-side in Machu Pichu!

Was in a chocolate chip cookies recently and spotted a nag called 'Swanton Blue' and can't for the life of me understand why Neil Diamond sprang to mind, although apparently it's backed heavily by the Chinese because they think it's 'Wonton Soup'! Saw another one named 'Mukhateer' and wondered if it was in relation to those three

French blokes or yer man from Birkenhead who used to eat blind Scouse and played for Ahlind 'Yer johkkkkkin' ahrn't yer?'!

While watching Gaelic football, a guy bounced the ball twice before continuing unpunished. One of the lads said 'That's a free out'. I responded 'Jayziz, there was even more 'hops' than a group of Nineties ravers on pogo sticks in a Vietnamese minefield'! 'Yeah, even more 'hops' than Irish dancers using stepping stones to cross a crocodile-infested river visiting the creation of House 13', said he'!

Heard a bloke once say he wished he was a fly on the wall. Now he's a bit of a messer this fella so not if I had a can of insecticide and a tea towel he wouldn't!

Spotted a horse called 'Lihou' one day. Is that anything to do with 'laughs last laughs longest'!

A pundit once described a horse race as being 'A game of cat and mouse'. Surely it was a race of horses and jockeys, right?!

A guy says to another 'You don't look like you're from around here'. 'Well, do you think I might look like his distant relative Over Yonder', he retorts. Needless to say egos can come to the fore in certain places when scenarios like this happen!

The referee for the 2019 Champions League Final was a gentlemen called 'Skomina'. We Liverpool fans could petition Skoda to name one of their new models after him for awarding us that penalty in the first few seconds!

A newscaster on radio was reading out the weather reports at the end of a bulletin one time and mentioned something about 'Mist or fog'. I suppose he's closely related to Mr. Dents who's closely related to Mr. Drink Driver, ey?!

Heard a story of a musician who became so poor during the economic crisis a few years ago he became an 'Ordinary Decent Criminal'. Now, I've seen a fiddler on the roof, but listening to a fiddler on the fiddle now brings a whole new meaning to me!

Was watching boxing on television and heard the commentator say 'Ducks one way and then the other'. It was piddling rain outside too, so when he said 'Ducks', you'd have to be forgiven for wondering what precisely he was referring to if you're going to think that way, right?!

Saw a horse run one day called 'Oscaraldo'. His fav Eighties band were 'El Zorro Goes to Hollywood'!

My mate told me he ate beans on toast one morning, and when we were in the pub later his arseh*le sounded like it was trying to re-recorded the beginning of Mambo Number 5!

Cameramen were outside Jeremy Corbyn's front door one morning during 2017 when I spotted his garden had totally overgrown. 'Shirxit' obviously, do yiz reckon?!

Ever wondered what it would be like if you were unfortunate enough to be dyslexic trying to spell out the name of that 'Blah blah blah gogogoch' place in north Wales to a guy with a guide dog?!

Met a young American lad one day who said the group he was part of in university was called 'Delta chi ro (i.e. letters in the Greek alphabet)'. Wonder if he ever flew from the U.S. to the capital of Egypt at any stage afterwards!

A mile away, a family called Gunne with loads of kids live close-by to an old friend. 'I'm beside more Gunnes than the population of the U.S. after 1 a.m.', he quipped one day. 'Come to think of it, more people sleep with guns than those they want to make love to over there, don't they?', he concluded!

I'm sure some of you have been asked to take part in a 'Last Man Standing' football competition in a pub at one point or another. You'd be forgiven for thinking it was a drinking game of some sort though, wouldn't you? There might be a few who think they'd be able to drink themselves rat-arsed for just a tenner though, right?!

Was watching the Olympics a few years ago and noticed some of the women taking part in the hammer were so strong they could participate in an articulated lorry throwing with Jupiter on the back contest. I'm tellin' yiz, it's not only Pepperami that's a bit of an animal!

Spotted toilet paper with a 'Best before' date one time. 'Best before' pulling your jocks back up I would have though anyway, ey? But, at least it was scented in fairness!

My late dad (Lord rest him) put a mince pie in the microwave for fifteen minutes with the foil cup still beneath it one Xmas. Honestly, there were more sparks than R2D2 and CP3O trying to light fires to keep themselves warm on their descent from having conquered Mount Everest!

On getting her pail of water Jill sat 'next to Jack'. Come to think of it, my book sales account with my publishers show precisely that!

Drank a non-alcoholic beer that tasted like metallic cornflakes a while ago. It tasted so bad, it wouldn't even appeal to Jaws from those James Bond movies in my humble opinion!

Guy texts his friend 'What are you doing later?'. 'Getting myself a bucket and watching the UFC', he responds. 'Surely you'd eat it?', he asks. 'Eat the cage fighting?', he replies confusedly. His mate enquires 'Does UFC not stand for Utah Fried Chicken or something?'. Friend quips 'You're mad! Although, in fairness you'd certainly ruffle up a few feathers if you were to tell all those clucking Mormons they weren't the Salt Lake City of the Earthly, wouldn't you?'! 'Yeah', he says. 'It'd knock the giblets out of them alright'!

A mate said he lost forty euro in the bookies one time but had a good day. 'You had a good day?', one of the lads asked. 'Yeah' he continued. 'Normally it's one twenty'!

A barman told me a guy would drink me under the table. He died of liver cancer a short time later which means he only ended up drinking himself under the lid of a coffin!

Saw a horse called 'Andronic' run one day. Put 'Gin' in front of him and you'd get a popular drink...and the fact it was even placed would have depressed some I'd imagine!

An good African golfer doesn't know much about fore for Toutouh and when he plays football it's in a 4-4-2 too!

I'm sure people from Dublin are familiar with the surname 'Brabazon'. Wonder if that's a mixture of the fella released by Pontius Pilate instead of Jesus and a river in South America!

Seen a foreign last name 'Rondon' too. What you'd get if you crossed that clown out of McDonalds and a Mafia boss in the capital of the U.K.!

There's a local family called Maples where their son took a leaf out of his brother's book and went to live in Boston. 'Are you sure he hasn't gone to the front of the Canadian flag instead', quipped a neighbour!

Saw an African surname called Ja'afari one time and wondered if that is what religious Rastafarians go on when they visit places like Kenya!

Wonder if any of you can remember that lots of well-loved celebrities passed away during 2016. Thought to myself 'That GOD is cruel'. But, not because he's taken them all away, but because he expects warped people to keep on coming up with jokes about it all!

Came across 'adjacent' while flicking through a dictionary one day. Thought to myself 'He's associated with those argonauts, isn't he?'!

There's a guy I know who has a fear of Friday the 13th and gets time off work because of it. Why not just tell his boss he's afraid of Friday full stop and he'd only ever have to work a four day week all the time. Yeah, as if that'd be successful alright!

A mate asked 'What song is that playing on the radio?'. I replied 'And the Grass Won't Change Your Mind'. 'That's not true', says he. 'I heard smoking that stuff can give you schiz and sh*t', he retorts!

The old saying goes 'You are what you eat'. True. A young footballer I know had fowl so much for dinner during the summer, he ended the next season with fifteen red cards!

Two guys at a horse race meeting. One asks, 'What's the tote?'. 'Somebody cute who puts bread under de dill', responds the other!

A mate told me he jarred his knee. Didn't have the heart to say 'Would it not have been better off to pour a pint of Guinness into your mouth instead, no?'!

Was watching a game of football one day, and the referee must have given out more yellow cards than urine sample test centres of China!

Horse racing was on the box in my local during the afternoon of a weekday (rarely enough!) when a bloke said 'The McCains are good'. Says another Dub 'Listen mate, this is the nags. If I wanted oven chips, I'd go to the supermarket'!

Bought a packaged microwavable item in a convenience store one time when it had 'Pierce film' printed as part of the heating instructions. Now, what a bunburger has to do with James Bond movies is completely beyond me anyway!

Asked a friend what another was getting up to for an international soccer game when his reply text read 'He had a shower and a shave, now he's having a pint in The Bath (A bar near The Aviva Stadium, Dublin)'. I asked him consider his answer. We laughed!

Was trying to access a website, but wasn't allowed because I refused to accept their cookies. I tried to explain to my mates later I couldn't as I was off biscuits for Lent. There was no response from them surprisingly enough!

'One For Arthur' won the 2016 Aintree Grand National. Well, it was 1-4 Scousers at OT back on March 14th, 2009, wasn't it?!

The Pope 'canon'ises people every now and then. I thought 'What if they preferred to support Tottenham Hotspur instead?'!

There's a Welsh Conservatives political party called 'Dyfodol'. Are they those yellow flowers that begin to sprout up in around the time of the Cheltenham Horse Racing Festival?!

A sports news channel said a football manager 'rules out buying frenzy'. Would somebody mind telling us all who's this 'Frenzy' fella is anyway and what position he plays?!

Spotted a horse called 'Tartini'. Is that, that stuff 007 had shaken along with vodka in those flicks I wonder?!

Paddy says to Mick, 'Took the pledge and kept it until I was eighteen as a young fella'. 'Jayziz, your oesophagus must have been totally dust-free for quite some time so', he responds!

The name 'Girralytis' makes me chuckle. It's probably what you'd find if you Googled the medical term for 'tennis elbow'!

A friend got the Eir sports package, but moaned there were 'Lots of empty channels'. 'About as much on it as a naturist at 250/1', quipped another!

Glasgow Celtic played Astana a few years ago. Didn't she sing 'All Kinds of Everything' for Ireland during the 1970 Eurovision Song Contest?!

A league in English football were sponsored by 'Vanarama'. Weren't they that girl band that sang 'Venus' and all that back during the 80's?!

Watched the Manchester derby in The Concorde one night and thought I heard the commentator say something along the lines of 'United wouldn't want to go 'gung ho' at it'. Walking home afterwards, I popped into The Lemon Tree, went up to the counter and the conversation with the assistant went as follows: 'Give us a House Special Gung Ho with egg fried rice please...and could I have it with extra cashew nuts if you wouldn't mind as I'm going to be sharing it with my favourite Chinese prostitute and her pet panda who had a movie named after him also, mate'!

I don't mean to sound too much like that gentleman from Dublin who wrote a tribute song to the Hillsborough disaster and retired it after the twenty fifth Anniversary Mass, but I decided to put a poetic analogy up on my Facebook page one hundred and fifty five months to the day since my beloved Liverpool F.C. last won the F.A. Cup and I wanted so much to put a '1' in front of the number of me gaff. It was also thirty four years to the day since Ronnie Whelan scored an equalising goal versus Manchester United in an F.A. Cup semi-final at the Gladwys Street end of Goodison Park…and I sincerely apologised that I couldn't hold off for that day next year as a tribute to the second highest possible check-out in the game of darts!

Was in a coffee shop here in Dublin recently when a girl wearing a 'California' t-shirt ordered a Chocca Mocha Americano. Wonder if he's that fella from the East Side who represented Cuba in the super heavyweight division back during the 1984 Olympics?!

Like me, there are a lot of 'Christians' who believe The Second Coming of Christ is not far off and that His Bride should be preparing herself. All I will say is, is that I hope Liverpool isn't a 'Forgotten Town' and Jesus doesn't come up off The Bridle of that white horse of His too soon otherwise He may not get by 'Many Clouds' and cross the line first in the Aintree Grand National during an April!

A Facebook post from March, 2019: 'Happy International Women's Day. Actually, I've just learned it's tomorrow because they've changed their minds. Oh, now I'm hearing they've decided it's next Tuesday, Wednesday, Thursday and Friday because Cheltenham is on and men will be enjoying themselves'!

…and another Facebook post of mine from the following week during March, 2019: 'Well, today is Gold Cup Day and the final one of this year's Cheltenham festival. Hope you have all had a great time watching it and made yourselves a few quid. Now, I have a deep voice, and even in comparison to Lee Marvin (Lord rest him) singing 'Wandrin Star', make him sound like a tenor, but talking about tenners, if I lose any more of me b*llix, I think I'll be in a position to do an audition for The Vienna Boys' Choir! Enjoy and soak it all in peops'!

Was talking to a man before who told me a young footballer wasn't going to make a professional career out of the game because he was a 'boozer'. Have to say I found that humorous as you'd hardly describe a hypochondriac as being a doctor's surgery, now would you?!

The Cedar Lounge, Raheny got a 'Birra Moretti' tap fitted. Looking at this tap, I think that must be the bloke who obviously went on to create a brand of beer after becoming AS Roma's all-time top goalscorer a few years back, right?...'He shot. He scored. His beer will be adored. Moretti. Moretti'!

Thought this one up while having a pint one day during early 2019, but don't know if it's original. Irish bloke walks into a coffee shop during Italia '90. Barista asks 'Can I help you, sir?'. 'Give us a cafe 'Au lait. Au lait, au lait, au lait. Au lait. Au lait'', says he!

Saw a horse run in the Middle East around the same time called 'Baroot'...so now I see that, that boozer on St. Assam's Ave in Raheny has its' origins in the Lebanon...and think of their national flag too!

Have any of you ever spotted that Dutch football team 'Go Ahead Eagles'? Well, I tell yiz all, they lose so often, by the end of fixtures, I'm sure it must have crossed their minds at some stage they should re-name themselves 'Finished Behind Turkeys'...'Birds of the Nether can't cross for a header'!

A Facebook post of mine from early 2019: Have to say I really like the way some groups in Northern Ireland are lobbying for the lowering of the alcohol content in beverages. So long as it tasted more or less the same, I'd happily sip away on my favourite drinks with somewhere between 0.5 and 1%. Now, Paddy's Day is not long away, so I hope some people go easy as the PSNI could be about, enter a premises after hours and the patrons would have to climb onto the roof where it might make the front page of 'ON PUB LOCKED'!

While on a working holiday in the United States during the early Nineties a restaurant I was employed by were selling a cup of coffee for 25c. A customer made a complaint about its' quality. A colleague reacted 'Well, why not getter better for $1?'. The man said 'Hmmm'. The owner of the establishment retorted 'You wouldn't spend four quarters at The Super Bowl on a free ticket you miserable jerk'!

A football commentator remarked a 'ball produced very little' one time. I thought 'Well, it obviously wasn't the fella who had a testicle removed and shacked up with the young virgin who lived in a shoe'!

I can be very mysterious, but there's this bloke I once knew who was about as easy to understand as it would be to listen to a cover of 'Informer' by Snow being sung in Dutch by a Glaswegian on karaoke when he's pissed off his head!

Was listening to the song 'My Friend John' by Those Nervous Animals, and figured the vocalist sounds like he's singing out his nose. Well, at least that's better than talking out his arse, isn't it?!

Overheard an auld fella in a pub referring to 'A load of hullaballooh' one day. Is that the capital of Hawaii I thought of asking him?!

A statistics caption on a sports channel showed 'Chelsea 3-4 Hull' which was all about shots on target. Thought to myself that was like an album by The Housemartins and that those Cockneys have obviously caught up somewhat since the Eighties!

Saw a goal scored during a soccer match one time during Winter with a shot that was so hard, the 'keeper could have caught a cold. Can almost imagine the back page tabloid headline 'BLEMsip'!

The people in my local Italian chipper are great people, but sell so many snack boxes, surely they could be the Siccini family. And by the way, Siccini is not what Sicilian women wear at the beach when it's warm and sunny!

There's a football club in Italy called 'Crotone' which could be those bread things you put in minestrone soup and that. While 'Pescara' could be that stuff women put on their eyes when getting ready to go out at the weekend, right? And lastly, the Greek side, 'Iraklis', could be in relation to that that medal thing Roman Catholics get blessed with holy water when they go on pilgrimages to places like Fatima and all that!

Have any of you ever figured that the Welsh surname 'Llewellyn' could be the name of the character who married JR in Dallas!

Made a point while watching a game in the pub one night when a friend said 'I agree with you' despite a number of others disagreeing. On seeing the replay I said, 'I've seen it again, I don't even agree with myself so you're all on your own on this one, mate'!

The staff in my local boozer are very obliging and often boost the power in my mobile phone, but honestly, there are even more 'chargers' in the place than the police forces of Los Angeles and the history of San Diego!

Any of you who may be old enough might remember the drama 'The Thorn Birds' which was shown on television during the early Eighties. Drogheda was pronounced 'Drugeeda', but is that not that Girls' National School near the Garda station in Raheny (on the north side of Dublin)?!

A bloke asks a guy in the chocolate chip cookies. 'Any tips?'. 'Yeah', he replies 'if it's over fences, don't back Buckeroo'!

I do go 'on the dry' for January. Yeah, 'dry' roasted peanuts along with my pint of beer/lager that is!

There's a song by Paddy Casey that says 'everything must change' so often, the only thing that's not changing is the lyrics in the fecking song!

A U.S. President once said he and his Canadian counterpart 'have a lot of common ground'. Well, North America is a rather large land mass in fairness I suppose, ey?!

There was something on Irish news about a 'Whistleblower to Tusla' one time. Hold on, there's a song about being only twenty four hours from that place, isn't there?!

Spotted the surname 'Basta' a while back. Is that, that stuff Italian people with bad head colds eat along with bolognese sauce and all that?!

Paddy asks Mick what song is playing on the radio. 'Does My Ring Hurt Your Finger', he answers. 'That's what I proudly enquired to the nurse while having me prostate checked last week', says he!

Paddy says to Mick he was out on Howth Hill and 'Nearly got blown off'. 'Didn't realise there was a red light district out that way', he responds! 'Saying things like that can come back to bite you on the mickey', he rips. 'You'd swear you wanted a part in the re-make of 'Cross of Iron' is Mick's attitude!

More than just on the odd occasion have I heard a football pundit say that a missed chance 'was put on a plate'. Listen, John the Baptist's head was put on a plate, but I bet the woman who received it didn't think it had just come out of the microwave piping hot, presuming it was still covered in stretching seal and didn't know where to stick the fork like the striker obviously did by missing an opener!

Heard of a bloke who was discharged from St. Ita's, Portrane just after there was a breakout of influenza in the place one. 'One 'Flu Over, The F*ck Who's Next?', ey?!

People do laugh at us Irish when we go abroad and the sun is beaming probably because they know we couldn't get a 'Tan' if reading the local telephone directory while lying on a sunbed at the beach during the height of Summer in Kuala Lumpur!

Came across a website during 2019 that said 'Action not supported'. You'd be forgiven for thinking they were referring to a football team having being forced to play behind closed doors, would some of yiz not agree?!

Heard a story of a boy who was asked to leave a church choir as: 'He wanted to sing at Mass about as often as there'd be a blue moon when Christmas Day fell on Good Friday at the turn of a millenium when the Second Coming of Christ was occurring'!

Wonder if some of you witnessed the Samoan haka on television during the 2019 Rugby World Cup in Japan like I did. By the way, think I saw some of those moves in a Janet Jackson video a few years back...and just because they play in the same colours as Italy, what's with the fungul @ the end of it too?!

'Boys From The Black Stuff' was on the B.B.C. during the early Eighties. Honestly, I don't know what Scouse brent geeses' arseh*les must have been made of back then at all at all, but it must be of some sort of metal given what stout was like outside of Ireland back then!

It was raining so hard here in Dublin one Winter's day, I even had to move on some whales who were congregating and getting a bit rowdy, drinking '20,000 Leagues Under The Sea Lite' outside my front gate. All they had to say was 'F*ck off, The Man From Atlantisgogogoch'!

I once heard a business analyst say he was long copper. Sounds like a scene from 'Days of Thunder', don't yiz all think?!

I turned forty eight on Dec 13th, 2019 and come the next day, I promise I didn't feel a year under forty nine!

Saw a banner at a Liverpool football match just after Rafael Benitez left the club that read 'TA RAFA LA'...is he not that bloke who played goalkeeper for the Brazilian national soccer team back in the Eighties and Nineties, no?!

I wonder if any of you have ever found it as puzzling as I that people from Glasgow are Glaswegians, but the citizens of Moscow are not referred to as Moswecians...or maybe even Glasgovites the other way round?!

Once heard a bloke say 'I'll take myself off somewhere'. Felt like retorting to his friend 'Hey, Somewhere. He can do an impersonation of me if you wants to too, mate'!

Was watching AFC Bournemouth playing Tottenham Hotspur in London at the end of November 2019 when I spotted they had more Wilson's than McGurk's in Howth!

If any of you are ever looking to be exposed to a little toilet humour, you should tune into the Bloomberg Channel as every so often they mention something about the CAC's dropping!

Have to take the opportunity to get my own back on a famous Monty Python sketch which frustrated me greatly as a teenager by bringing up the fact that country people here in Ireland call Dubs 'The Tonys' as they should be aware lots more from Dublin travel to Merseyside to spectate at football matches because they are of course...Liverpudlians not Evertonians!

During January, 2020, it was reported that some bloke by the name of Klimala had arrived to sign for Glasgow Celtic. Sounds like a cross between the ex-lead singer of Kajagoogoo and what people from the Far East would call an Eighties female body spray, do some of you not think?!

That 'Rate My Plate' Facebook page really can be very funny when you read some of the comments on the various dishes concocted and posted. My contribution to the debate one time was in reaction to a rather dodgy-looking Shepherd's Pie to which I said "Little Bo' wouldn't even 'Peep' at it let alone tuck in'!

Paddy and Mick are having a pint together in their local. Barmaid walks by and says to Paddy, 'How's your back, arseh*le?'! 'Well, you'd hardly expect him to have a front arseh*le, now would you?', says Mick having the craic!

Just like we gave birth to Christmas Day and St. Stephen's Day, I really think so much money gets spent on Black Friday it should be followed by Skint Pink Saturday with it being the Jewish Sabbath and all that says this bald fella who's partial to the odd polar neck jumper!

Anyone who has ever known me would know all about my love and affection for the City of Liverpool and its' people when 'Love Me Dooh' by The Beatles came on the radio one morning, and I spotted a horse running at Angers in France called 'Gicky D'amour'...and I'm sure the United fans as well as Scousers will p*ss themselves at that one!

My mates played football with a bloke called 'Moses' who scored away from home so many times, I honestly actually think he'd forgotten all about what the sixth commandment asserts!

Apparently, water bottles in your front garden stops dogs from having a sh*te there. Now, I'm no animal psychologist, but I reckon the reason they refrain is because they are saying in their minds to themselves that if they dump their cylinder there, that's what sized one will be shoved up their arsesh*les should they do so as punishment!

Spotted a horse called 'Two in the Pink' one day and thought is that anything to do with burying your baldy fella when you have diphallic tetra?!

A woman mentions to her husband that men were encouraged to seek disciplines that repressed the way they were sexually programmed, and then turns to him several minutes later and tells him she 'was gagging for a sausage in batter after winning an inflatable banana at the bingo'. Talk about something backfiring!

A doctor said he'd heal a patient, but it would be 'a slow job'. He enquires 'Is that not what you'd go to a prostitute for instead, no?'!

Was flicking through the channels during the Summer of 2019 when I decided to stop at the EWTN as they were quoting a Scripture passage that says something along the lines of anyone who eats and drinks and doesn't consider the body, being liable to judgement. That's fair enough, Yahweh. Whenever I go for a few pints and the chipper afterwards in the future, I promise to think of that famous picture of Elle MacPherson in her swimsuit and let it linger in my thoughts for at least a while. Absolutely no probs whatsoever mate!

Some females are interested in joining the priesthood and I will admit I could be quoted as saying albeit as a joke that in that case they are transvestites, but I reckon I'm even more accurate in saying there are a lot of men who dress in kilts that are more than just a little fond of a bit of skirt!

Paddy and Mick are having a pint together over the Christmas period of 2019. Says Paddy, 'That Van Dijk is outrageously good, ey?'. 'I know', Mick replies and continues 'Playing alongside him even I'd have a great chance of winning the Ballon D'or and even at my age too'! 'Yeah, but with a beer belly like that I doubt it', retorts Paddy. 'Okay, what about the Ballon Dutch Gold then?', quips Mick!

Would somebody mind telling me if the song 'Last Christmas' is all about what Ebenezer Christ advised The Three Wise Men we had if The Second Coming occurred at 00:00:01, January 6th, 1 A.D....and the twelve days is all we ever had in the first place?!

My beloved Liverpool F.C. became Club World Cup champions just days before Christmas 2019. But, honestly, when was the last time the bloke with the winner got booked for taking off his top when celebrating on the Pope's instructions as the Third Secret of Fatima is written all over his upper body!

...and I heard the Advocate was shown a vision while he was sleeping approaching the Christmas of 2019, and in it in beautiful, shining golden figures it was revealed to him his number is *777*!

Printed in the United States
By Bookmasters